The Things I Learn

I Learn from My Grandpa

Lorraine Harrison

illustrated by
Anita Morra

PowerKiDS
press.

New York

Published in 2018 by The Rosen Publishing Group, Inc.
29 East 21st Street, New York, NY 10010

First Edition

Managing Editor: Nathalie Beullens-Maoui
Editor: Greg Roza
Art Director: Michael Flynn
Book Design: Raúl Rodriguez
Illustrator: Anita Morra

Cataloging-in-Publication Data

Names: Harrison, Lorraine.
Title: I learn from my grandpa / Lorraine Harrison.
Description: New York : PowerKids Press, 2018. | Series: The things I learn | Includes index.
Identifiers: ISBN 9781538327135 (pbk.) | ISBN 9781508163763 (library bound) | ISBN 9781538327838 (6 pack)
Subjects: LCSH: Grandfathers–Juvenile literature. | Grandparent and child–Juvenile literature.
Classification: LCC HQ759.9 H383 2018 | DDC 306.874'5–dc23

Manufactured in the United States of America

CPSIA Compliance Information: Batch #BW18PK. For further information contact Rosen Publishing, New York, New York at 1-800-237-9932

Contents

I love being with my
grandpa. He teaches me
lots of new things.

4

My grandpa likes to make things.

He teaches me to make things too!

We're going
to make
a kite.

We need two sticks, paper,
and some string.

10

Grandpa teaches me how to fly the kite.

The wind helps it go high.

It starts to rain.

My grandpa says rain comes
from clouds.

Grandpa and I like to paint.
We paint a picture together.

We paint a picture of Grandpa's house.

I learn how to mix
colors together.

17

We made a pretty picture.

We let it dry near the window.

The table's a mess.

My grandpa teaches me
how to clean up.

My grandpa is the best teacher!

Words to Know

mess

rain

window

Index